Buried Treasure

by BRIAN TRUEMAN

Book version by Nicholas Jones

*Illustrations from the Cosgrove Hall production
Directed by Chris Taylor*

THAMES METHUEN

First published in Great Britain 1985
by Methuen Children's Books Ltd
11 New Fetter Lane, London EC4P 4EE
in association with Thames Television International Ltd
149 Tottenham Court Road, London W1P 9LL

Copyright © 1985 by Cosgrove Hall Productions Ltd

Book version © 1985 by Thames Television International Ltd
and Methuen Children's Books Ltd
Printed in Great Britain
ISBN 0 423 011405

The unabridged edition of THE WIND IN THE WILLOWS
by Kenneth Grahame is available with full colour illustrations
from the award-winning Cosgrove Hall production.

The Cosgrove Hall film of the original book
by Kenneth Grahame is available on Thames Video

Buried Treasure

The Wild Wood is not a friendly place for those who don't know it. The great trees trap the sunlight, and only a few shafts reach the ground on the very brightest day. Even the birds do not venture deep into it, and the spongy earth seems to soak up noise as readily as it does the rain. But there are paths, and in the daytime, with the proper passwords and signs – and perhaps with a stout stick lest anyone bars your way – then it's possible to journey safely along those paths, to Badger's house, set in the finger-like roots of an oak. He's not an animal who particularly likes company, so the Wild Wood suits him well. A journey there is always worthwhile, for the welcome he'll give to his friends is as warm as the earth outside is cold. Mole knew this, and had confirmed it that very morning when *he* made the journey. He was still in Badger's comfortable parlour when there was a knock on the door. Despite Badger's genuine delight in visitors, however, his reaction to such an intrusion was always the same: 'Yes, yes, yes,' he would mutter, shuffling to open the door. 'Now, what is it you w——' He broke off in mid sentence when he saw who his visitor was. 'You!'

Had his visitor been another friend – Ratty, for example – his tone would have instantly mellowed. But seeing a *Weasel* on his doorstep . . . !

The Weasel was undaunted by his welcome. He had the confidence of knowing something the other didn't. 'Yes, me, Mr Badger!'

'And what might you want?'

Mole called from the parlour: 'Badger! Who is it, Badger?'

'It's the leader of those ruffianly Weasels!'

'Now, now, Mr Badger! That's hardly polite!'

Badger ignored the protest. 'I have nothing to say to you or your kind, as you well know. I must ask you to leave.'

'No, no, no, Mr Badger!' The Weasel continued unabashed. 'No, you got it all wrong. *I* must ask *you* to leave.'

Mole had come to the door now, and couldn't contain his indignation. 'How dare you talk to Badger like that!'

The Weasel sneered a reply: 'Oh my goodness! Ain't we a blooming hero – when we're with our *friend.*'

Badger was above such pointless argument: 'Look, say your say and get you gone,' he instructed.

'My say, Mr Badger, is 'ere. My say says that this "ruffianly Weasel" has bought a piece of land. *This* piece of land. Bought it and paid for it.'

Mole was incredulous. 'Bought a piece of . . .'

'A piece of the Wild Wood,' the Weasel con-

firmed. 'This 'ere piece wot used to 'ave Mr Blooming Badger's 'ome in the middle of it.'

'Used to have!' exclaimed Mole. Badger asked, less impulsively,

'Just what are you saying?'

'I'm saying my say, Mr Badger. I'm telling you as we owns this land, and we own's what's on it. I'm saying that you have to go, and there's the proof of it.' And the Weasel waved a legal-looking document beneath Badger's nose, just slowly enough for Badger to make out that it was, indeed, a title to property. Could the Weasels really have managed such a coup? For almost the first time in his life, he was lost for words.

'But, er, but I . . .'

Mole, not held back by Badger's suspicions, was more definite. 'Just get off with you. Get . . . get back to your own kind. Ju . . . just . . . go!'

The Weasel merely laughed. 'Ha, ha, ha, ha! I'll go. I'll go. But I'll be back three days from now, Mr Badger, at noon. Three days from now. Ha, ha, ha, ha!'

As the Weasel departed, Mole exploded. 'I never heard such impudent nonsense, Badger! I don't know why you didn't see him off.'

But Badger didn't immediately agree, and Mole began to sense that things were perhaps not as simple as he had assumed. 'Badger? It's all right, isn't it?'

'I don't know, Mole.'

'Oh, Badger!'

'I'm no lawyer, Mole. There's only one place to find out who has the right, and that's in Court.'

'In Court? Oh, Badger!'

And so it was, two days later, that Badger stood before the Magistrate. Word of the events had spread, and the Court was crowded. All the evidence had been heard, and Mrs Carrington-Moss was summing up:

'. . . and although we are cognisant of the implications herein,' she concluded, 'the Court finds this Deed of Property is a valid legal document.'

The Weasels burst into gloating jubilation. 'Ha, ha, ha! We've done it!'

The Magistrate tried to restore order. 'Please! Court!'

There was little effect. She decided a sterner approach was necessary, and banged her gavel on the desk.

'If I hear any more rowdyism from the recent purchasers of a certain piece of the Wild Wood, I shall have them charged with contempt of Court, riotous behaviour, several breaches of the peace, and occasioning actual bodily harm to an officer of his Majesty's Court of Law, viz giving me a headache.'

The Chief Weasel did not intend to tempt either Providence or the Magistrate after his victory, and put on his most ingratiating tone:

'I'm, er, sure I 'umbly begs your Worship's pardon, on behalf of my naturally over-excited and exuberant colleagues, your Worship.'

Mrs Carrington-Moss, if the truth be told, was sorry that she had to interpret the law as she did, and was disappointed that the Chief managed to quieten his followers so quickly. She added:

'If it happens again, it will be many years before you're able to enjoy your victory in this Court.'

'It won't happen again, your Worship.'

'O. O well, in that case, Mr Badger, you have only one line of defence open to you. That is the possible existence of an earlier Deed which would establish your legal right to possession of your present home. Er, does any such document exist?'

Badger could only sigh. His meaning was clear, and Mrs Carrington-Moss asked encouragingly:

'Are you sure?'

'Quite sure, Ma'am.'

'Well in that case, I'm very much afraid, Mr Badger, that I have no option but with regret to reject your Appeal against the notice of eviction served upon you.'

Badger's acknowledgement was drowned by a great burst of cheering from the Weasels. When it had died away a little, the Chief confirmed:

   'It's noon tomorrow, then, your Worship?'

   'It's noon tomorrow.'

*   *   *

Rat and Mole would not leave things there. Next day, with many of the Riverbankers and Wild Wooders who had been in Court, they went to Badger's house. 'And if the Court says that Badger has to go,' Rat pronounced, 'then it's taking sides with the Weasels, and if it's taking sides with the Weasels, then it's wrong. And if it's wrong, then I say we ought to fight it, and fight the Weasels too.'

The crowd had gathered round. They approved vigorously.

'You see, Badger,' added Mole, made confident by the cheering. 'We . . . we won't let you be turned out. We won't let you.'

'Hmmm. Er, it's no use Mole.'

Ratty was not certain about the rights and wrongs of the situation, but he wanted to cheer Badger up. 'Now look here, Badger old man . . .'

'It's no use, Rat. You cannot fight the law.'

'But dash it all, Badger . . .' Ratty exclaimed.

'The law is the law, Ratty. When the Weasels are wrong, the law protects us. When the Weasels are in the right, the law protects them. I have lived by the law all my life, and I'm not changing now.'

Mole had calmed somewhat, and decided to try persuasion.

'Badger. All these Wild Wooders. They, they . . . love you. We all love you. How . . . how can we just stand by and . . .'

But Badger was firm: 'No! No. I'm grateful for your friendship – for your anger – but it's no use. Now, go back to your homes, and leave me in peace. Leave me.'

Ratty led the Wild Wooders out. Mole remained with Badger who soon asked,

'Have they gone?'

'Only outside, Badger. They'll want to . . . see you off.'

'Dear friends . . . *dear* friends. You know, Mole, my family has lived here for hundreds of generations – before the Normans came, before the

Vikings sailed up Rat's be-
loved river, when a great
thriving city flourished here.
But for all that, it's more my
friends I'll miss than the fire-
side.'

Mole was overcome. 'O,
Badger!' he sobbed.

'And now, I think, my
friend, that I'd like to say
goodbye.'

'But . . . but . . . why, Badger, there's an hour or
more before it's noon.'

'No, Mole. Not to you, but to my home, and my
father's home. Home to the badgers for so many
years.'

'Oh, ah . . . Yes. Of course. Of course, Badger.'
Mole moved away, leaving Badger musing to
himself.

'Dear me! He, he! What would my father say?
What would he say?'

Mole thought he'd better do something practical to keep his mind from the sorrow of the occasion. 'Shall I see if you left anything in the other rooms, Badger? Or in the cellar?'

Badger was deep in his own thoughts. 'Mmm? Ah. The Cellar,' he mumbled vaguely. 'Yes, yes. That would be most kind, Mole. Thank you.'

Mole wasn't sure if Badger had really heard him, but the search would give Mole something to do, so he set off, leaving Badger to sigh to himself,

'Aaah! Who's to curb your wilful ways now, young Toad? Tch, tch, tch, tch!'

*　　*　　*

Mole began to explore. There were no end of passages and tunnels, with enticing little rooms off them. Badger's home was larger than Mole had ever realised. Some of the darker, more distant rooms were a little frightening, Mole had to admit – but he wanted to be sure that Badger had not left anything behind, any momento of these happier days in his ancestral home. He found that Badger had done the job very thoroughly. There was

nothing but the usual few pieces of rubbish – the kind of thing which always seems to remain when you've cleared a room (how well Mole knew that from his own spring-cleaning!). But then, in one of the darkest and most distant tunnels, almost lost in the drab stone of the tunnel wall, Mole saw something glint. He looked a little closer, and . . . yes! A door handle! He turned it. It was stiff, very stiff.

He pulled the door slowly ajar. A room? Surely not. 'No. Just a cupboard of some kind,' he said, aloud to himself.

'And nothing in there, either.' He took just another glance in the dim light. Maybe . . . Maybe there was something there, though. 'Uh. Yes. A box of something. Um. Maybe just a box of nothing. Still. Better take it upstairs,' Mole said encouragingly to himself.

He struggled back with it – an intriguing carved box, about a foot long and nine inches wide. It would be something to keep Badger's mind from the approaching deadline, anyway.

'Here we are, Badger,' he said brightly, as he returned to the parlour. 'Just this box and . . . Badger! The fire's almost out!' Mole stopped aghast. In all his many visits to Badger, there had never been an empty grate in the parlour.

'O, the fire. Mmmm. Not worth keeping in. Not worth keeping in.'

'But Badger,' remonstrated Mole. 'I'm . . . I've never known it to be . . .' The full force of what was happening hit Mole. 'Ooh, Badger!'

'O, come now, Mole. This won't do. What have you got there, eh? Gold pieces? Ha, ha! Have I been as rich as Toad all these years and never known it?'

'I don't know, Badger. It's a dusty old box.'

'Well, let's open it. Here. Here on the table. It must have been down there for years.'

Mole peered inside, and announced, disappointed, 'It's just a piece of paper.'

Badger wasn't quite so sure. 'Or something like paper.' It looked more like parchment to him. Mole tried to make out what was written on it.

'Goodness!' he exclaimed. 'What funny writing!
"Hoc documento . . . melibus acu——"'

'Good heavens, Mole! That's Latin!'

Mole wasn't sure that he knew what that meant.
'O.'

Badger, on the other hand, was delighted. 'The
language of the Romans!'

Mole began to understand why Badger was

excited. 'You mean the people who built all these passages . . . the . . .' Was it *that* old? 'The . . . people who were here all those . . .'

Badger, however, wasn't just thinking about how old the documents were. One word had caught his attention. 'What was that word again? "*Melibus*"?'

'Yes . . . Er . . . "*documento melibus*".'

'But that means . . . Let me be sure now. Where's my Latin dictionary? Where did I pack my . . .? Ah ha! Here it is.' Badger paused as he riffled through the pages. 'Now . . . "*medulla*" . . . "*medius*" . . . here: "*meles*" – a badger!'

'A Badger!' Mole exclaimed.

Badger began to translate words on the parchment – for that's what it was. 'O, bless my father for making me stick to Latin,' he remarked as he began. 'Now! . . . "*Hoc documento* . . ."" – By this document . . . "*melibus* . . ."" – that'll be "to the badgers" . . . and to their heirs . . . for, er, taking . . . is transferred all the land described hereinunder for ever.'

'O, Badger, what does this mean?'

'It means that someone . . . Let me see . . . ah, "Cesare"! Ha, ha! It means that Caesar, Julius Caesar, gave this land to the badgers for ever. Ah! O, Mole!'

'Oh-h-h, Badger!'

As they realised just what this meant, both animals began to smile. Badger remembered Mole's earlier distress at seeing the fire fading to mere embers. Things were different now. 'Can't you see that the fire's nearly out!' he said jokingly.

*   *   *

Outside the door, the Weasels had returned.

'This is Weasel property. We got a legal document. And you ain't,' the Chief was shouting. 'You're trespassers, the lot of yer!'

Ratty did not know of Badger and Mole's miraculous discovery. He was worried only about keeping the dignity of the law. 'This *is* Weasel property,' he agreed. 'You shall have it. But it's not yours for ten minutes yet.'

The Chief Weasel was scornful. 'Ten minutes! Ha, ha, ha! Ten minutes!'

His Henchman could see no cause to worry about such details. 'I say we takes it now!'

Some of the Weasel rabble advanced towards the door. But Ratty was still on guard. 'Stay back!' A scuffle began. The last five minutes up to noon looked like being an unseemly scramble, but Badger came to his door and shouted imperiously:

'Stop! Stop it, all of you.'

The Weasels knew of old that it was unwise to fight Badger, and they slunk away, taunting, 'Five minutes! Five minutes, Mr High-and-mighty Badger, and the law says it's ours!'

'The law! Yes, yes. We must live by the law,' agreed Badger, apparently conciliatory. Ratty was horrified: 'Badger!'

Badger continued his reasoning. 'Surely you see, Rat, how the Weasels have reformed?'

Rat could not understand how even a Badger downcast by having to leave his home could be so tolerant of those who were about to force him out. 'Reformed!' he exclaimed.

'Mmmm. They're not the double-dealing, hypocritical, bullying villains they were.'

The Chief Weasel, although pleased by this apparent praise, could not let such a description pass. 'Here, steady on!'

'They are law-abiding citizens!'

'Eh? Ah?' The Chief couldn't quite see what Badger was leading up to, but he had to agree. After all, the law had given them the right to this land, had it not? 'Yeah! That's right!'

Badger continued his argument: 'When the law says I must go, I must go.'

The Weasels began to chatter amongst them-

selves. Was Badger really going to leave his home so peacefully?

'And when the law says I must stay, I must stay.'

The Chief had no patience for such things. It was noon. 'Very interesting, Mr Badger. You know, I loves a bit of philosophy myself, but now, if you don't mind . . . Come now, Mr Badger, the law is the law . . .'

Badger produced his trump card: 'And the law says I must stay.'

Ratty was not expecting this. 'The law, Badger?'

The Weasel wasn't expecting it either. 'Come off it! Come off it! We 'ad this out in court. This says you must go!' He waved his Deed in Badger's face.

'And this says I stay!'

The Weasels broke into cries of outrage and fury. Ratty could scarcely believe Badger could have found the proof he was seeking. 'Badger, what is it?'

'An ancient document, found by Mole, written by the Romans.'

'The Romans?'

'And giving the badgers this home of ours for ever.'

The Chief Weasel began to wonder if there might be something in it, after all: 'Ere. Lemme see——— let's have a look at that! "*Hoc documento*——". Tch! I don't believe yer!'

'The law is the law,' said Badger, matter-of-factly.

'The law!' sneered the Chief.

'And you are law-abiding citizens. You bought my land when it could not be sold.'

'You——' began the Chief, but Badger cut in:

'. . . And now you can leave it!'

The Weasel realised he had been outmanoeuvred. Not even he dared go back on his admission. He had used the law when it suited him, so what could he do now? 'I'll get even with you for this. You, you . . .' Words failed him. There was no point in continuing the discussion. 'Come on lads!'

The Weasels trooped raggedly away. Rat turned to Badger. 'O! O, Badger!'

Badger turned to Mole: 'Mole, my friend. I am forever in your debt.'

Mole's could think of no adequate reply, so said instead, 'I . . . I think we ought to get a kettle on that fire of yours.'

Rat and Badger laughed at Mole's practical suggestion. 'Good old Mole.'

They went inside. The crowd outside Badger's door had witnessed all this in delighted silence, not wishing to miss a word of the exciting developments. Now, they laughed and cheered. Badger would be safe in his home for ever.